Twinning Twosday

"Summer Before Middle School"

Abby's POV

Written by

Desiree and Elisa

Publishing Company

Copyright ©2024 by Desiree Fleming Revised
originally published ©2020 Desiree Fleming

ISBN: 978-0-9841797-7-0

Published in the United States by EJF Publishing

Table of Contents

Chapter One

"Silver Shoe Box"

Gabby and I, "Abby", were born on September 2, and our family adored the day we arrived. Our mom and dad had so many matching outfits, shoes, and head bonnets for us.

Our grandmother, Globessie, helped my mother care for us from infancy until we entered preschool.

As we grew up, Gabby and I attended the same daycare and elementary school, sharing the same classrooms. We were exactly alike in many ways, but we were totally different in others. We are actually fraternal twins.

Take me, for instance. I love to sing, play sports, and hate long fingernails and nail polish; anything too girly is a no-go for me. I prefer hanging out with boys, wearing high-top gym shoes and baggy clothes. And did I forget to mention? I have straight red hair and hazel brown eyes.

Gabby, on the other hand, has curly blonde hair, blue eyes and hates sports. She loves ballet and playing the flute. When it comes to clothes, she adores wearing her cute dresses with the cutest little high-heel pumps every day. To finish her look, she loves her fake nails, brightly polished.

Ever since I could understand that Gabby and I were twins, I couldn't grasp why our mom always dressed us alike every day from the day we were born. Mom always put the cutest hair bows in our hair; at the end of the day, she'd wonder what happened to mine. She didn't know I was removing them and hiding them in a little shoe box in my closet.

Gabby and I couldn't be any more different than two left shoes! The way we learned things at school just highlighted that. I always struggled with math, and Gabby had a tough time with language arts. Strangely enough, in the areas where one of us found difficulty, the other excelled.

On the last day of 6th grade, right before summer break, Mom was in our bedroom, cleaning out drawers and replacing winter clothing with summer wear. To her surprise, she found the cutest little shoe box in the closet.

"Hmmm," she wondered, "Could this be a gift for me?"

She didn't want to open it and ruin a surprise, especially since her birthday was coming up. But she couldn't resist.

She reasoned that we would never know. So, she opened the shoe box. To her surprise, she saw over fifty hair bows of all colors—the very bows she had put in our hair from kindergarten through 6th grade.

Later the same day, before Gabby and I arrived home from school, Mom placed the black and silver shoebox in the middle of the kitchen table where she served our after-school snack. We could not miss it. How would we react to seeing she had found the secret hidden stash of hair bows?

Gabby and I walked in through the back door. As I hung my backpack on the hook in the mud room, I overheard Mom. "There's an extra snack today."

Being the last day of school, we were ecstatic. Neither of us noticed the black rectangular shoebox placed on the table until...

Mom said, "The bonus snack is inside the shoebox I found in your closet."

Gabby replied, "Oh, cute box!"

Standing there with my mouth wide open, all anyone could see were my tonsils in the back of my mouth; I couldn't believe Mom had found my hidden shoebox.

Mom said to Gabby, "I love how you keep up with your hair bows." Then she turned to me. "Hey Abby, where are yours?" I couldn't get a word out.

Gabby quickly chimed in, "Yeah, where? Come to think of it, you come home without your hair bows every day."

I was furious with Gabby for bringing up the bows, especially since Mom had discovered my hidden box.

"Okay, Mom! You got me! It's my shoebox. But I hate wearing those big, bright hair bows. Gabby and I have been dressing alike since forever! I just wanted to dress differently."

"So, you don't like dressing like me?" Gabby asked.

"No, it's not that, Gabby. I just want to be different. Look at us; we already look different. My hair is straight and red, I have brown eyes, and my face is browner than yours. You, on the other hand, have curly blonde hair and blue eyes. Your skin is a little lighter, and you're taller than me. The only thing we have in common is that we both like the same color. So why do we have to dress alike? We already know we are twins, right? I just want to be myself, that's all," I explained.

"You've got a point, Abby," Gabby admitted.

"Now, Abby, I totally understand you want to be different. But you could have told me instead of hiding your hair bows. I love seeing my little beauties dressed alike, but I would've considered your feelings about being yourself. Since you told the truth, I am going to give you an option," Mom said.

"An option?" We were curious.

"Yes, an option. I will allow you to dress as you choose in Middle School, with the understanding that every Tuesday, you and Gabby will dress alike."

"Twinning Twosdays! I love it, Mom!" Gabby was excited.

"Twinning Twosday! No! NO! NO!" I shouted.

"Well, the other option is back to the hair bows," said Mom.

"Okay, Mom. I'll do 'Twinning Twosdays,'" I replied, grumbling under my breath.

"Okay, Mom. I'll do 'Twinning Twosdays,'" I replied, grumbling under my breath.

Chapter Two

"One Condition"

Yes, the first day of summer break. I was extremely excited knowing sixth grade was behind me, and my summer was about to be lit. I was up bright and early, playing music through my headphones, singing every song that played. I was dancing and singing, wearing my oversized pajamas, walking around in our big pink and purple bedroom, and belting out some of my favorite songs. I was super excited that I had 70 days off school before middle school. I was determined that my first day of summer would be the best-memorable-day-ever. I texted my friends Ryan, **(my crush)**, Brett Stevenson, and Camille to come play me in a game of basketball every day, after breakfast. I knew nothing could possibly get in the way of me enjoying my first summer before entering middle school.

Gabby, excited about having the opportunity to sleep in, hit the snooze button on the alarm clock three times. When she woke up, she heard me just a singing.

"Why are you up so early and singing?" Gabby asked.

I didn't say a word. Gabby pulled the blanket over her head and turned towards the wall, attempting to go back to sleep. My singing seemed even louder than before. Gabby pulled the blanket over her head, sitting on her bed, now screaming.

"Why are you up so early and singing so loudly?" she yelled.

I still didn't say a word. But my singing kept getting louder and louder until Gabby couldn't take it any longer.

"Hey!" Gabby yelled out. "What's going on? It's 7:30 a.m. Are you nuts, singing like you're in a rock and roll band!"

Still listening to my music, I couldn't hear Gabby. So, she got out of her bed, popped me in the head, and asked.

"Why won't you answer me?"

"Ouch! Why did you hit me in my head?" I cried.

"Because you kept ignoring me," Gabby said.

"Yeah, well, sorry! I have my headphones on," I replied; I didn't know you called me."

"Oh really! You aren't sorry." Responded Gabby.

You're always '**crabby Gabby**' on the first day of summer," I said. Anyway, Mom is cooking breakfast.

"I knew I smelled Mom's homemade biscuits and turkey bacon," said Gabby.

"I'm going downstairs to get my food," I told Gabby.

Gabby felt pretty bad about popping me in the head. She thought to herself.

"Am I really crabby, every year on the first day of summer? Well, so what if I am? It's my first day to sleep without having to do any school work. Now, where is my comb and hairbrush? I know I remember leaving it on the dresser last night. Abby must've moved it. She can't keep up with anything. I'm going to get my comb and brush," Gabby said.

As Gabby walked down the stairs, she thought to herself, "I couldn't possibly hear my mom and Abby discussing math, or do I?"

The closer she got to the kitchen; her assumption was proven to be true. Mom was showing me a math problem on a math website.

Gabby inquired, "What's going on here? I must be dreaming. I mean, it went from Abby singing her lungs out at 7:00 am to 7:30 am, to me walking into a kitchen classroom, could somebody tell me if I'm awake?"

"Good morning, sweetheart; well, you are awake, Gabby," said her mom.

I interjected, "Gabby, I have some good news and bad news. What do you want to hear first?" Gabby said, "The good news." "Well, the good news is it really is summer and you really are awake."

"Okay, okay, what's taking so long to get to the bad news?" reluctantly asked Gabby.

"Well, the bad news is Mom read our report cards, and it reads that I have to take math this summer in summer school," I said.

"GEESH! That's not bad news for me, that's bad news for you. I thought you were going to tell me I had to go to summer school," smirked Gabby.

"I wasn't quite finished. Your report card shows that you have to take language arts in summer school," I smirked back.

"This isn't fair! This isn't fair!" cried Gabby.

"I know, but if we don't, there will be no middle school for us. So, I'm going to need your help with my math," I said.

"No, no, no! I don't want to be in summer school. Help yourself!" shouted Gabby.

As Mom walked out of the kitchen, I began to tell Gabby what Mom said.

"Mom says we can't go outside until we do these practice problems on the website, and I want to go outside because my friends are coming to play 'around the world' basketball with me. Please, sister, do your work," I pleaded.

"On one condition," replied Gabby.

"Yeah, what's the one condition?" I asked.

"You have to dress like me today and during summer school," said Gabby.

"Are you kidding?" I asked. "How can I play basketball in your little high heel pumps and frilly dresses? Nope! Not doing it. I can't play ball like that, and you know it," I cried.

"Well, we see who won't be going to middle school this fall," laughed Gabby.

I gave in to Gabby's condition to get help with the math work, wearing Gabby's cute little purple high heel pumps and dresses as a blouse. Gabby took so many pictures of me playing basketball in a dress and pumps. I was upset with Gabby all weekend.

Chapter Three

"Third Floor"

Monday morning, I dreaded getting up. I just knew my days at Lexington Elementary were completely over, for the rest of my life. As I lay in bed, I tossed and turned with dreadful thoughts of getting up on a sunny summer morning, not to go outside to play basketball with my friends, not to go fishing down at the creek, nor to just sleep in and do nothing. I prayed, "Jesus, please let this be a dream."

Then my mother called my name, "Good morning, Abby."

I said, "Yes, God answered my prayer."

"You're going to be late for your first day of summer school. Your sister is down here fully dressed and eating breakfast. What's taking so long?" stated my mom.

I started kicking my legs under my purple blanket, pulling the covers over my head, grunting, "I don't want to go. I don't want to go. Why do I have to take math again?" I cried.

I started thinking of one of my brilliant ideas, as I always do.

I thought to myself, "I know what I'll do; I will just pretend that I hurt my ankle playing basketball yesterday. Because, I know my mom isn't going to want me walking up all those three flights of stairs just to do math in that old rickety building, especially since there's no elevator. Yeah, that's exactly what I'll do. I'm going to get up and limp down the stairs."

As I limped down the stairs, Gabby was approaching the stairway and said, "Morning, Abby, why are you limping this morning?"

"I hurt my ankle yesterday," I replied. "When? How? We were together all of yesterday, you didn't get hurt," said Gabby. "Yeah, well, I hurt it after church," I grumbled.

"Ouuuweee, you're making up a story, you must be up to one of your 'most brilliant ideas' again. I'm going to tell Mom you're trying not to go to summer school today," said Gabby.

"No! Don't do that!" I said.

"And... tell me why I shouldn't tell Mom you were going to lie and trick her today?" Gabby cunningly replied.

"Who cares, I'm not going, anyway," I frustratingly replied.

"Ooh Mom!" sang Gabby.

"You better not!" I said.

"I won't tell her only on one condition," said Gabby.

"Geesh! Another condition! What one condition?" I asked.

"I won't tell Mom you were planning one of your schemes; I meant 'brilliant ideas,' trying to trick her to get out of going to summer school," said Gabby as she was abruptly interrupted by me.

"A scheme? A plan to trick her, are you serious?" I questioned.

"Yep! Ooh Mom!" sang Gabby.

"Okay! Okay! What is the condition, this time?" I asked.

"Well, you have to do Twinning Twosday with me every week of summer school," said Gabby.

"What, uhn uhn! Every Tuesday! NO! I'm not dressing like you, you're crazy," I yelled.

"Ooh Mom!" snickered Gabby.

"Fine! This is so wrong, but... okay, I'll dress like an old lady," I rolled my eyes. "I'll only do it so you won't tell Mom."

Later that morning, after arriving at Lexington Elementary School, Gabby and I split up and went our separate ways. Gabby headed to the second floor for Language Arts, and I continued up to the third floor for math. I had to walk up three long flights of stairs to get there.

The closer I got to the third floor, the more I thought I was hearing a familiar voice. I thought I heard my old 5th-grade math teacher, Mrs. Catchaback. The closer I got, the more distinct the voice became, and then the daily school bell rang.

"Awe Naw, please, please don't let that be her. Oh no, it sounds just like her. Mhhhmhhmhhmhhmhm... that best not be Mrs. Catchaback, because if it is, I'm gonna faint or run out. She's one of the tallest ladies I've ever met, with the slowest walk, that missing tooth in the front, red lipstick wearing, the loudest and slowest talking voice, always wearing those big orange and brown worn-out shoes, with the same blue jean pants and green turtleneck sweater, even on the hottest days, every single day and always saying she thinks someone is thinking," I thought.

Just as I turned the corner to enter the third floor, there she stood, standing 6 feet tall, red lipstick, wearing those small red reading glasses on the top of her nose with the chain hanging from them, in the doorway greeting students, with that one tooth missing and her messy bun—I do mean messy—with her big orange and brown shoes, blue jean pants, and green turtleneck sweater, in this 90-degree weather, Mrs. Catchaback.

When I looked at Mrs. Catchaback, I turned around and ran. Mrs. Catchaback said, "Get back over here, Abby."

"Yes, Ma'am," I said as I dreaded the first day of summer school, I just about fainted.

I couldn't believe I was back in a 5th-grade classroom. Mrs. Catchaback welcomed the students to the 6th-grade summer school, encouraging us to find a seat of our choice. Mrs. Catchaback didn't care too much for change; she kept her classroom set up the same way the entire 30 years of teaching. The white walls in her room turned tan through the years. Her bookshelves were stocked with dusty, outdated books, and the sound of the creaking desks could be heard all the way down the hallway as students adjusted themselves in their seats on unpolished, squeaky hardwood floors. Mrs.

Catchaback never liked getting rid of anything because she always felt that "someone might need this someday." She never changed anything and dressed exactly the same all 30 years of working at Lexington Elementary.

"Students, did you bring your pencils and some loose leaf paper? It's going to be a looooooong two hours of summer school. But, if you're ready to go to middle school, I'm sure you brought everything you need with you. If not, look into my green shoebox on my desk and get what you need, but you must return my pencils; I might need it later," she looked at me as she said this.

"I hate this class. How did I end up again in the same class with Mrs. Catchaback?" I thought.

"I know some of you are wondering how you ended back up in my 5th-grade classroom for summer school. Don't worry about it," said Mrs. Catchaback.

"This is going to be the worst summer ever," I thought.

"I'm sure some of you think this will be the worst summer ever, and guess what, it will be," shared Mrs. Catchaback.

I thought to myself, "How does Mrs. Catchaback always know what I'm thinking?"

"I always know what you're thinking," responded Mrs. Catchaback.

It was just my imagination thinking Mrs. Catchaback heard my thoughts. The truth is Mrs. Catchaback couldn't hear my thoughts; she just responded to what she thought kids were thinking.

"She must be a witch," one of the other students thought.

Mrs. Catchaback replied, "For those of you who think I'm a witch, I'm not. Now, let's get back to summer school.

"It will be the worst summer because, had you passed 6th-grade math, neither you nor I would be here. Nevertheless, let's get on with your summer learning," said Mrs. Catchaback.

Mrs. Catchaback wrote a math equation on the old chalkboard.

"Who would like to come up to demonstrate what you know? Seeing that there are three of you, I'll help you choose. Come up, Abby!" called Mrs. Catchaback.

"Out of all the people in this room, why in the world did she call on me?" I thought. As I dropped my head on my desktop, trying to practically drag myself out of my seat.

Mrs. Catchaback said, "I'm sure you're probably wondering why I called on you, right?"

"How does this lady know what I am thinking? This is really getting creepy. I'm not sure how much more of this I can take!" I mumbled.

"Ok, show me what you know. I'm sure you should remember something from class when I subbed for your teacher. We went over this just about four weeks ago," insisted Mrs. Catchaback.

I started thinking about what was going on with me about 4 weeks ago. I thought to myself, "Maybe I should tell her the truth. Sorry, Mrs. Catchaback, I wasn't listening. Actually, I was goofing around with my friends. My mom has been telling me to tell the truth lately, so there's the truth! Nah, she could not handle the truth." "Mrs. Catchaback, I went to my dentist appointment and must've missed that week because my mouth was so sore from my deep cleaning."

"I hope you don't say that you missed school that week because I remember sending all of your classwork home along with your twin sister, Gabby," said Mrs. Catchaback.

I was about to run out of the class. I couldn't imagine how my teacher was always one step ahead of me.

I thought to myself, "I can't believe Mrs. Catchaback is so much worse than she is during the school year. How does she know everything I'm thinking?"

After my first day of summer school, I knew this was going to be the longest three weeks ever, and I could not wait to walk home and talk with my sister Gabby. On the way home, I couldn't get a word in, as Gabby couldn't stop talking about how well she did on her first day. She continuously bragged about how the teacher had her help other students in the classroom with their summer school work.

Gabby asked me how my day went.

I embarrassingly replied, "Oh, it was, I mean I was, well, it was more than I expected; I meant it was a very interesting first day, if I have to say so myself! I can't wait to go back tomorrow. We don't need to keep talking about summer school, let's get on with our fun afternoon. Because, as you know, we'll be right back there tomorrow. I can't believe we have summer school class Monday through Thursday for the next three weeks."

"And to think this was just the first day," said Gabby.

"Well, I can't wait until it is over," I mumbled.

"Did you say something?" asked Gabby as she was walking down the sidewalk, running her hands across the red picket fence.

"No, it wasn't that important, I guess you'll get the last laugh this summer," I replied.

"Yep! I guess you could say that," replied Gabby.

Chapter Four

"Out Of Order"

The smell of bacon, grits, and biscuits wafted under our bedroom door. Mom was up cooking, as she does every morning. But her early bird, me, hadn't come down for breakfast yet.

As the alarm clock was going off, I refused to get up. I thought to myself, "Why did this day have to come so quickly? I just fell asleep, well, at least it feels that way." I was very depressed, knowing I had to get up, get dressed, and head to summer school.

Eventually, I got up to get ready for school. Gabby just stood there, watching me drag around slowly, as if she had nowhere to go and nothing to do. As I pulled my jogging pants and t-shirt out of the drawer, Gabby cleared her throat saying to me,

"Excuse me?"

"You're excused. Why are you saying 'excuse me' when you're way across the room!" I replied.

"Have you forgotten what day it is?" Gabby asked.

"Forgotten? How could I ever forget what day it is? It's another boring lecture with Mrs. Catchaback! Ooh, can't wait to get out of summer school," I exclaimed sarcastically.

"Right, but it's also a special day," Gabby said.

"Gabby, it's not our birthday, so what else could be so spectacular about today?" I frustratingly questioned.

"Today is Twinning Twosday; how could you possibly forget that?" Gabby stated.

"No, no, no, not today, Gabby! This is not fair. I have to deal with Mrs. Catchaback today. How about we wait until summer school ends?" I screamed.

"Oh, Mom!" sung Gabby.

"Okay! Okay! You win! What are we wearing today?" I asked regretfully.

Gabby responded, "I'm so glad you asked. I have this pink and green dress picked out just for you, look at these beautiful flowers."

"Flowers??.....NOOOOOOO!!!!" I screamed.

"Ooh, Mom!!" sang Gabby.

"Okay, what else?" I asked, reluctantly.

"I also have these polka dot purple tights," Gabby said.

"Purple tights! I'm not wearing any purple tights in this heat; my legs will melt, especially not with polka dots," I shouted.

"They will not melt. You just need to walk slowly because these orange heels you're going to wear with them will help you walk more ladylike," Gabby snickered.

The nerve of my sister taking advantage of my weakness. How dare she want me to look like a decorated Christmas tree at the top of the summer? She knows it's going to be 98° today. How am I going to bear walking to school in those ugly orange shoes, let alone those hideous hot polka-dot purple tights? She could not possibly love me... And my friends, what are they going to say if they see me... My God!

This is probably going to be the worst summer day, ever! I just hope I don't see my crush, because if he sees me like this, he will think I'm all girly and probably never play basketball with me ever again. I can't risk him seeing me like this. I'm going to have to hide my face while we're walking to school. I can't be seen looking like Gabby, it's an embarrassment!

After we got dressed and finished breakfast, we headed to school. I decided to wear a big straw hat to cover my head and face as much as possible. All you could see under the big brown straw hat was my nose peeking out; you couldn't even see my eyes.

Gabby was having such a great time talking and chatting with me along the way that neither of us ever noticed a huge pothole in the middle of the sidewalk that wasn't there the day before. BAM! Out of nowhere, I tripped over the pothole, falling flat on my stomach and face, scraping my knees, putting a hole in my hot purple polka dot tights, with one foot stuck in the pothole. My dress came over my head, and wouldn't you know it, as Gabby was helping me get my foot unstuck from the pothole stood Brett Stevenson, with his bluish-green hair, bouncing his basketball a few steps past the pothole.

He looked down, asking if he could help me up, not noticing it was me. I was mortified, disguising my voice like an old lady, I handed Brett my left hand, all while holding my hat down towards my face, as I got up, out of embarrassment, saying, "Thank you, Sir," hopping down the street with one shoe on my foot and the other in my hand. Brett thought to himself, "That old lady really does put me in mind of Abby, but nah! I know she would never dress like that, although it's kind of cute."

I hoped Brett didn't figure out who I was. I was in total disbelief that he literally saw me, in a dress and tights on a hot summer day.

We didn't stop running until we arrived at the school. As we approached the school building, I forgot all about Brett, realizing I had to walk up three flights of stairs, not noticing my left shoe heel had broken off, and had to deal with Mrs. Catchaback, all over again.

I dreaded walking up those long three flights of stairs, not to mention the school was extremely hot. I was sweating so badly, I took the bottom of my dress to wipe the sweat from my forehead. As I started walking and limping up the stairs, one by one, one at a time, I started sweating again, as if I were on a beach in Florida in the hot sun. The closer I got to the third floor, the more I cringed as I heard Mrs. Catchaback greeting the other two students. My legs were sweating so bad that those purple tights felt like someone had placed a heater by my legs, I thought to myself, "my legs feel like they're on fire."

I was sweating pigs by the time I made it upstairs with no air conditioner, and the old school building didn't make it any better. My mouth was as dry as the Sahara Desert, I cried out "Water."

Mrs. Catchaback said, "Abby, you should've gotten water on the first floor before arriving at class. Didn't you see the Big 'OUT OF ORDER' paper on the water fountain when you left yesterday? You walked right past it."

I couldn't believe Mrs. Catchaback's response. I was extremely agitated, I thought to myself, "Doesn't she see this water drenching from my face? I could die of dehydration."

I then asked for a water bottle, as I was visibly in need of some water.

I thought to myself again... "Can't she see the sweat running down my face? I really need WATER." Mrs. Catchaback wouldn't let me get water when I was visibly dehydrated with sweat running down my face."

Mrs. Catchaback handed me a water bottle and said, "Here you are, I don't want you to dehydrate."

"Not another one of these days," I thought. Afterwards, Mrs. Catchaback said, "I'm sure you are wondering if this is going to be another one of those days, and it is because it's another learning day. I would like to know who did their homework last night?

Oh, I forgot to tell you all, turning in your homework helps us to get out of summer school quicker. Instead of having three weeks of summer school, we can be out of here by the end of next week but you have to turn in all of your homework."

"Homework!" I thought. "I barely did my homework during school. How am I going to have time to do homework on summer break, play basketball with my friends, and go fishing? My summer is now ruined, for sure! I know Mrs.

Catchaback had my teacher fail me in this class on purpose, just so I could miss my summer fun. This is so not fair."

"I know some of you feel it isn't fair to have homework during the summer, and under normal circumstances, you would be right. But trust me, it is fair," Mrs. Catchaback explained, pointing at the three students. "Had you done your work and homework during the school year, none of us would be here right now. So, in order to go to middle school, you must pass 6th-grade math. I advise you to take notes, ask questions, and do your homework."

I began to feel a little stressed, unable to imagine not going to middle school with Gabby, realizing there was no way for me to understand summer math, seeing how I had failed math during the school year. I thought to myself, "If only I had a tutor, but Mrs. Catchaback is just too mean."

"Just in case any of you want a tutor, let your parents know; I tutor on the weekends as well, though I do charge an additional fee," Mrs. Catchaback told us.

"No way! I'd rather wear this dress with these hot tights for the rest of my life than have tutoring with Mrs. Catchaback. Hmmmmm... Gabby is very good at math. She passed her 6th-grade math."

My confidence in passing my math class went through the roof, figuratively speaking. I just knew Gabby would be willing to help me. After all, I was dressing like her today.

After math class was over, I couldn't wait to get downstairs to talk with Gabby. But unfortunately, Gabby had an awful day in class. She thought that every day would be that way because the first day was just about language arts games. When I saw her walking out of her classroom, she was gleefully smiling, as she approached me.

"How was class?" I asked.

"I hate it and never want to go back to summer school ever again!" Gabby cried.

I started thinking, "This is not going to work; neither of us is doing well in class, which means neither of us will get to middle school." Shouting out loud, "Oh no! Not another school year with Mrs. Catchaback."

"Another year? What are you screaming about, Abby?" Gabby asked. "What's that look in your eyes? I've seen that look several times, and it always gets us in trouble," she said.

"I have an idea!" I said.

"I don't want to hear any of your ideas."

"I'm going to tell you anyway."

"Your ideas always include lies, and I'm not going to be part of your plans full of lies," Gabby said.

"Well, I guess I'll tell Mom you've been bribing me to do this Twinning Tuesday with you," I threatened.

"No, don't tell on me, Abby; I don't want to get into trouble. What's your brilliant plan?" Gabby asked reluctantly.

"What about we switch places for the next two weeks?" I suggested.

"No can do! I will not," Gabby responded firmly.

"But, Gab, think about it. If we both fail our summer classes, we both have to repeat 6th grade and do every subject we passed and redo these summer classes," I explained.

"You do have a point there, Abby. But we look nothing alike," Gabby replied.

"Look at us today; we look just alike," I said.

"Not at all! Just because you have similar outfits doesn't make us look alike in the face. I mean, look at our hair and eyes; what about our complexions and heights, Ms. Genius?" Gabby shouted.

The thinking wheels began to turn in my 6th-grade mind, planning my most brilliant plan.

"I have it all figured out, Gab," I shouted excitedly. "Do you remember when Mom went to the 70's party with her friends, and they all wore different wigs? Well, Mom's friends gave theirs to her for us to wear for our costume party when we were in 4th grade."

"And what is that supposed to mean... Oooh... I'm listening," Gabby replied.

"Mom has a couple of wigs left in the attic. I remember seeing a curly blonde and straight red one."

Gabby just nodded in disbelief, knowing there was no way we could wear the wigs and get away with it.

"You can wear the red one, and I can wear the blonde wig," I said.

Gabby questioned, "Ok Ms. Brilliant, with the big ideas. You have a plan for our hair; what about our eyes?"

"Well, what about our eyes?" I responded.

"Duh, have you looked at our eyes lately? Yours are hazel brown, and mine are blue, dummy," Gabby said.

"I'm not a dummy... dummy, let me think about it!"

Gabby reminded me of all the times we got caught whenever I had a "brilliant plan". She remembered a time we were in kindergarten and I wanted the last 3 chocolate chip cookies out of the cookie jar so bad that I ate them and replaced them with my toy chocolate chip cookies, not realizing our old grandmother would want some later. Remembering the loud cry of her poor grandmother after biting on the metal cookie, breaking her two front teeth. I reminded her just how young we were and how I now have better thought-out plans. I just knew whenever I get to thinking, I'm working on a scheme master plan which could potentially get us caught.

"YES!! I got it! I got it! What about contact lenses?" I replied.

"Contact lenses! For who? For what?" Gabby shouted.

"Yes! Contact lenses, colorful contact lenses. That's what we need to change our eye colors," I exclaimed.

"OMG! Use your brain? I guess you're not!" Gabby replied.

"Can you be smart for just a second? In Dad's bathroom, remember he has color lenses; you know how he likes changing his eye colors," I shouted.

"Oooh, I see now," Gabby said.

"Okay, quiet down. Can you hear the watery squishy sound?" I asked.

"Not really... actually, I do. What's that hideous sound?" Gabby replied.

"That's Mrs. Catchaback, slowly walking down the stairs. Her shoes make the most awful squishy sound, like water and mud are in her shoes, yuck! Let's go, hope she didn't overhear us."

But, before we could leave the building, Mrs. Catchaback had already made it down to the first floor, standing leaning over the first step, adjusting her little square glasses, as she talked to us. "Abby, I meant to say nice outfit earlier, but you were sweating so profusely, I forgot to mention it. You and your twin looked so much alike today. I need to get a new eyeglass prescription, and you almost fooled me," complimented Mrs. Catchaback.

Gabby and I looked at one another and knew my plan would surely have to work.

Chapter Five

"Crossed"

As the week progressed, Gabby and I had been making lots of adjustments to be ready for our test day. I found the wigs in the attic, and Gabby found the contact lenses. We had the best time changing our eye colors, stuffing my sweatshirt so Gabby would look like me, and adding a cushion in Gabby's cute little pumps so I could feel comfortable. Mom thought we were having a makeover party with all the fun we were having. Little did she know, we had a plan to get into Middle School by any means necessary.

The next morning, I was up very early, working on the finishing touches of the wig I would wear.

"Ouch! That hurt... why did you hit me?" I shouted.

"Hit you? I didn't hit you, well not on purpose," Gabby replied, "today is our test date, don't you remember?"

"Nooooo!" I replied sarcastically. "Of course, I do. That's why I have mom's wig ready to put on and Dad's contact lenses, right here on the dresser. Let's get dressed," I said.

"Okay, but what if Mom notices?" Gabby cried.

"What if she doesn't!" I replied.

"Abby, if Mom sees us she's going to know who's who," Gabby responded.

"Actually, she's our first test, then Dad. Remember what Mrs. Catchaback said last week, she thought I was you. If neither one of them notices, we know our teachers won't notice," I explained. "Okay, so let's get dressed and let's get breakfast before Dad leaves for work."

As we prepared to go downstairs for breakfast and our parent test, Gabby crossed her fingers the entire time I was fixing the wig on her head, hoping, wishing, and praying they wouldn't get caught. She knew if we got caught, we'd miss the entire summer break on punishment. There we were walking down the stairs, and I assured Gabby everything would be just fine.

"Morning girls, toast for anyone?" asked Dad.

"Good morning, Abby and Gabby; summer school is almost over," Mom hugged us.

"Abby, you look a little taller today," Dad noted.

"Yes, and Gabby is looking a lot like Abby today," Mom added, trying to think of something quick to say.

Gabby said, "Oh, it's probably because we've been hanging around each other so much during summer school."

I could not let that statement from Gabby get us caught up, so I said, "Well, Mom and Dad, we are twins, don't you know. I mean, look at us, her hair is red and straight, with her brown eyes of course you know that's Abby and look at me I have my blonde curly hair with my blue eyes I'm Gabby. Abby would never dress like me," I explained.

Gabby was so nervous she crossed her fingers, legs, toes, and eyes; she just knew our parents were about to bust us.

Their mom looked slightly concerned, as if something wasn't right.

"Even your voice sounds a lot like Gabby, Abby," Dad explained. "If I didn't know any better, I think you girls were trying to play a trick on us today."

"Mom and Dad, if we don't hurry out of here we're going to miss our test today. Love you," I hurriedly replied.

"Yes, you are so right, girls. Do great in school. Make sure you take this piece of toast to eat on your way. I don't want you girls to be hungry while testing today. I know you're excited you have 7 more weeks to be out of school when summer school is over," Mom quickly responded.

"Then onto middle school you go," said Dad.

"I hope we get to go," Gabby grunted.

"What did you say, dear?" Mom questioned.

"Oh, I just said let's get ready to go, okay let's go Gabby, I mean Abby," I confusingly replied.

Mom did a double take looking at the both of us, looking a little more concerned when she overheard me call Gabby by her real name.

"Gabby, did you just call Abby, yourself?" Mom asked.

"You know, Mom, you're right, silly me, I am Gabby, right? I just got so confused with all this talk about us looking alike this morning and this test. I'm sorry, you're right. Come on (hesitantly) Abby let's go (Right NOW!). See you later, Mom. Have a great day at work, Dad," I hurriedly kissed them and ran out.

Chapter Six

"Doubles"

Mrs. Catchaback was in her classroom very early this particular Thursday morning, preparing the math summative for her three students. She was a very imperturbable woman; you couldn't get her upset or excited, she was just even keel. Students always knew what they could expect when entering her classroom.

But, for some reason today, she decided to add one math problem to the test to get the students to stretch themselves. Most students disliked Mrs. Catchaback, whereas others admired her calm demeanor.

She had seen many students come and go to 6th grade. She had some favorites and some she was thrilled to see move on to 6th grade. Mrs. Catchaback didn't get many visitors, but every now and again, an old student or parent would stop by to say hi.

A surprise guest came to see Mrs. Catchaback; she hadn't seen this person in over 15 years. She could hear the sound of what sounded like squishy water and mud mixed together in the hallway. But she couldn't quite figure out who it was approaching her door. She asked who it was, as she really needed her eyeglass prescription changed.

Mrs. Catchaback was totally shocked when her unexpected guest came into her classroom. It was her former student dressed just like her. She removed her glasses and put them back on, but she could not see what was standing right before her. Understandably, there stood Tabitha Digsby-Higgins, just as tall as Mrs. Catchaback, with a missing front tooth, wearing red lipstick, tiny red square eyeglasses, worn-out orange and brown shoes, with blue jean pants and a green turtleneck sweater, with a messy bun. Mrs. Catchaback passed out, falling straight back onto the hardwood floor, thinking she was cloned.

Tabitha ran into the hallway to get water, noticing the big "Out Of Order" sign. In a frantic panic, she grabbed the steel water bottle sitting on Mrs. Catchaback's desk, thinking it was water. This steel water bottle had been on Mrs. Catchaback's desk for the past 10 years, given to her by one of the parents as a parting gift. But, to Tabitha's surprise, there was rubbing alcohol in the bottle.

She didn't know that from time to time Mrs. Catchaback uses the rubbing alcohol to rub her swollen ankle down, in between classes and her lunch break. But, before smelling the scent, she'd already splashed a handful on Mrs. Catchaback's face. She woke up screaming deliriously so loud, as her face was burning; she thought her face was on fire, as the rubbing alcohol burned the heat rash on her face.

"What have you done?...... and Who are you?..... Are you me?..... Or am I me?..... Why are you here?..... Who are you? Have you come to take me back? Wait! Take me where? What am I talking about?" frantically said Mrs. Catchaback.

"Mrs. Catchaback, it's me, Tabitha."

"Tabitha Who? My face is on fire. Why did you burn my face?" cried Mrs. Catchaback.

"Mrs. Catchaback, it's me, Tabitha Higgins; my maiden name is Tabitha Digsby. I was the one; when I would think something, you always said what I was thinking, after I thought it," responded Tabitha.

"I don't remember," replied Mrs. Catchaback.

"Remember, I used to bring my frog to school in my lunchbag."

"Now, that sounds vaguely familiar."

"You always called on me during class. You were my teacher a little over 14 years ago. Don't you remember me?" responded Tabitha. "I don't remember you, I've had hundreds upon hundreds I've taught through the years. How can I remember you, out of all those students?" asked Mrs. Catchaback.

"Ok, remember when my frog got out of my lunchbox, and when you sat on your seat, he got in your sweater, hopping around your back?" reminded Tabitha.

"Oh my, that was one of the worst days of my teaching career. How could I ever forget Tabitha Digsby? Now that I remember that dreadful memory. Could you tell me why you're here playing this horrid trick on me, early this morning?" sighed Mrs. Catchaback.

But, before Tabitha could answer Mrs. Catchaback's question, Gabby, dressed like me, walked into the classroom. Her eyes opened as wide as the ocean; she passed out when she saw doubles of Mrs. Catchaback. She fell straight backward, bumping her head on the squeaky hardwood floor.

Both Mrs. Catchaback and Tabitha ran over to gently raise Gabby up from the floor, propping her on Mrs. Catchaback's dusty old wooden rocking chair. Tabitha went down to the nurse's office on the first floor to get an ice pack for "Gabby." As she was coming back to herself, she began rubbing the back of her head, wondering how she ended up on the floor.

Gabby got up, thinking she was seeing things, believing she must have just been stressed out, not knowing if she and I would get caught. After seeing that "Abby" was better and the other students had entered the room preparing to take the test, Mrs. Catchaback handed out the test so the students could take it. After the testing, the students turned in their test to Mrs. Catchaback.

Gabby, as "Abby," was so paranoid after testing that she couldn't wait to leave and switch places with the real me. She asked if she could be excused to go to the bathroom. However, Mrs. Catchaback noticed something different about Abby's voice.

She asked, "What's going on with your voice?"

"Oh, I have a...oh yeah...I have a summer cold, as she tried to talk in a more lower tone of voice.

I really shouldn't be talking because it hurts my throat when I talk," replied Gabby.

"Yeah, okay, but you look a little pale today, looking more like your twin Gabby, even more so than last week," exclaimed Mrs. Catchaback.

Pretending as if she were going to throw up, Gabby, as Abby, clasped her lips, holding her stomach, and motioning to go to the bathroom to Mrs. Catchaback.

"May I pleeeeeeease go to the bathroom? I feel terrible," begged Gabby.

Gabby ran down to the second floor; she couldn't wait to take off the wig and Abby's clothing. While changing out of the wig, contact lenses, and clothing, she was getting more nervous because I hadn't made it to the bathroom so we could switch clothes. Just as Gabby was about to put the wig back on, I came rushing through the door yelling...

"Come help me get these hot tights and hideous shoes off of my feet."

Gabby tried hugging me asking, "What took you so long?"

"I told her it's a loooooong story...you wouldn't believe it if I told you."

"Just try me," replied Gabby.

"Come on, we have to get back to class before the teachers wonder what's taking us so long," I replied.

We immediately ran out of the restroom; Gabby ran to her classroom and me up to the third floor to my classroom.

As I entered, after removing my wig and contact lenses, my eyes were a little irritated because the contact lenses were dirty. I didn't know about the "Double experience" Gabby encountered while in my class. I tripped over the steel water bottle left on the floor as I was walking towards my desk, bumping my head on the wooden arm of the old rocking chair. Upon getting up, Mrs. Catchaback walked over to see if I was okay, remembering I had fallen earlier.

As I was sitting up, Ms. Flanagan, the school nurse, came in. Tabitha was so out of breath she decided to wait until she could catch her breath and then head back up the stairs to Mrs. Catchaback's classroom.

Nurse Flanagan entered the classroom in a hurry, wearing her green nurse's scrub and an ice pack for both Mrs. Catchaback and me. As she bent over the chair where I was propped on the old brown wooden rocking chair, she heard me trying to say something to her. She asked me, "Abby, are you okay? Do you feel you need to go to the hospital?" I responded in a whisper, "Something must've gotten into my eyes or maybe it's too hot in the school because I couldn't see anything. I just fell over."

Just as she was whispering, in walked Tabitha, asking...

"Is she okay?" talking to Mrs. Catchaback.

I stood up looking at both Mrs. Catchaback's. My thoughts were completely confused... "I must be being punished because I cheated! Is my mind playing a game on me? Am I really here? Is this the right school?........... Why is Mrs. Catchaback playing this game on me? How are there two Mrs. Catchaback's?"

I couldn't imagine Mrs. Catchaback having a twin sister, dressed just like her. I just knew my eyes were playing tricks on me. I rubbed and rubbed and rubbed my eyes again, but nothing changed.

I began screaming "NOOOOOOOO!" and passed out, falling face forward.

Tabitha said, "I think I should just leave. I don't want this poor child injuring herself out of fear every time she wakes up. It was great seeing you Mrs. Catchaback, thanks for being a good teacher. When I went to college, I knew I wanted to be a teacher, just like you."

Tabitha and Mrs. Catchaback hugged before leaving out.

As I was beginning to wake up, I overheard Tabitha talking to Mrs. Catchaback as she headed out of the classroom.

I sat up thinking, "Who in the world would ever want to look like or be like Mrs. Catchaback? I know I wouldn't."

Mrs. Catchaback said to Ms. Flanagan, "There are a lot of students in this world who would love to be like me. I must be pretty awesome."

The nurse just smiled, not saying a word, as she couldn't understand who would dare want to dress like Mrs. Catchaback, either. Well, that's what I think she might've been thinking.

"I'm going to go call the ambulance to make sure Abby is okay," replied Ms. Flanagan.

"No, I'm okay; my head just hurts a little. Feels like a bump," I said.

"Yes, there's a bump. Do you feel dizzy? Let me help you stand up," Ms. Flanagan insisted.

As I stood up, the other two students helped out of concern.

I shared with Ms. Flanagan, "I'm fine. Plus, this is the last day of summer school, and I want to see my grades."

The school nurse left the class, sharing with Mrs. Catchaback and me to ring the hallway bell if I didn't seem to be myself.

Mrs. Catchaback encouraged the students to have a seat so that she could get started going over the grades for the final test they took.

I asked, "Mrs. Catchaback?"

"Yes, Abby, what is it? Also, you don't look as pale anymore. You look more like yourself," replied Mrs. Catchaback.

"Ok, thank you. But... who was the lady that was dressed just like you?" I asked.

"She was just an old student who reminds me a lot of you. She decided to become a teacher and wanted to be just like me," smiled Mrs. Catchaback.

"Yucky!" I mumbled.

"Pardon me," replied Mrs. Catchaback.

"Oh, nothing," I responded.

After the students sat down, Mrs. Catchaback told the students a long story about the importance of not cheating and why one should always be honest. The students didn't understand why she decided to have this talk today, of all days, seeing that the tests were already taken, and the grades from the pretest were, as well. But, I knew exactly why she was having this talk with us. I began to get very worried. I started biting my fingernails and thoughts began racing through my head...

"Does Mrs. Catchaback know Gabby and I switched places for the test? Could she really have found out? Does this mean I might have to repeat 6th grade all over again?"

Unbeknownst to me, as these thoughts were racing through my head, Gabby and her Language Arts teacher were coming upstairs to Mrs. Catchaback's classroom.

However, before they made it to the top of the stairs, Mrs. Catchaback began calling the students one by one, announcing out loud who passed on to the 7th grade. She called the first student up, handed him an envelope, and congratulated him on a job well done.

"You've passed on to the 7th grade," said Mrs. Catchaback. "You came to class every day, took notes, asked questions, and overall you did a great job."

As Mrs. Catchback continued talking, Gabby and her Language Arts teacher were approaching the second floor. Mrs. Catchaback called the second student up, handed her an envelope, and congratulated her on a job well done. She told her...

"Your work is outstanding. You paid close attention to every detail and even used your resources to come to me for tutoring during these past two weeks."

I furiously rolled my eyes at Mrs. Catchaback, knowing she would never say such a kind thing like that to me.

"Congratulations, you passed on to the 7th grade," said Mrs. Catchaback.

Mrs. Catchaback cleared her throat to call me up for my final grade. I didn't know how to react. I didn't know if Mrs. Catchaback knew I cheated and wanted to embarrass me in front of the class or if I really passed, maybe someone else cheated, too.

Just as I was walking up towards Mrs. Catchaback's desk, Gabby and her Language Arts teacher stepped into Mrs. Catchaback's classroom doorway. My mouth dropped, I felt as if I was having an out oof body experience. I could only imagine the only reason my sister and teacher were there was to tell about us switching to cheat.

As Gabby and her teacher entered the classroom, I said...

"Wait! I can ...I...I....can explain!"

Just then, the school fire alarm went off. Gabby, Mrs. Catchaback, the other students, the other teacher, and I exited very carefully down the emergency exit stairway. Once we made it outside safely and were all accounted for, Mrs. Catchaback looked at me saying...

"Now, what was that you were going to say, Abby?"

To find out what grade Gabby and I received on our summer school classes, get your copy of Twinning Twosdays "Middle School OR Nah?."

Twinning Twosday Quest-Connect Time.

1. What do you think happened to Abby and Gabby?

2. Did Abby tell the truth about cheating?

3. Do you think Mrs. Catchaback and the other teacher knew they cheated?

4. What was your favorite part of the story?

www.ingramcontent.com/pod-product-compliance
Lightning Source LLC
Chambersburg PA
CBHW070356120726
47909CB00008B/2875